Built on Broken

By Lelia Geppert

Built on Broken

ISBN: 9798365350519

Printed by Kindle Direct Publishing.

To the lost:

May we always be healing...

Cheers!

May 16, 2019

Graceless, she builds dreams
        without sleep;
Observing caterpillars morph
        into butterflies.
Ceaselessly reading minds,
        endlessly weaving tales.
She'll drink your pain,
        turn it to stone,
If only to heighten
        her imagination.

June 12, 2019

Altered sense of self-worth,

And alone, if not for words.

But low self-esteem's

Only the tip of the iceberg—

Not many can understand

Existing in perpetual suspense,

So I write to stop the ruse,

And regain my independence.

January 21, 2020

In the uneasiness

Of excruciating pain

Regenerating nerves

Fill my hollow soul

With fields of tulips

Red, blue, and white.

Unimagining the games I play;

Dimness, still, in the light.

January 28, 2020

Euthanasia wasn't an option,
And suicide could be a sin;

So he fought hell & high water,
Body overflowing with gin.

Until the day his heart finally broke
Though now he's at peace, again.

January 31, 2020

Arrangements made,

Obituaries already published,

And headstones chosen

For the lithe beings

Dancing around in my head.

Thin and graceful,

Weaving in and out of my body

As they please,

But I'll kill them with

Prescriptions' frightening ease.

I'm becoming accustomed to the
Company of a lithe, shadowy figure.
Often Found standing inside my window,
Peeking out behind the light blue curtains
—

Watching the outdoors for hours on end.
Maybe he's afraid to go outside.
I'm afraid he'll leave.

February 1, 2020

My mind's equipped with blue diamonds

Running through my veins.

I'd like to strike one of them

With a sharpened knife,

Just to see them spinning

Into red

           That will slow

When my mind stops

Making waves,

And ceases

Walking pavements.

Distorted dreams of reality

Different parts of things everywhere
Nothing in the right place

Deformed and traumatic

The reason I hate sleep.

(Co-written with @JarretNicholas).

February 3, 2020

Black sparrows in flight

Happily dancing

Racing to be the best

Fantasies to be lived

Their presence felt

Souls at rest

A simple fantasy:

To go with the wind,

Grow with the grain,

Magnificent, pearlescent—

Oysters never baked.

February 4, 2020

Unlike the simple

Hummingbird that dances

To complex music,

I'm frantically crashing

Like waves into a stone wall—

Atoms that have no where to go.

Frantically wondering

Which way is up;

Spinning into unconsciousness,

Or shock, I'm unsure which.

Clueless about what comes next;

Lost without your direction;

But in warmth and love

I go to sleep alone

With my thoughts.

February 5, 2020

Lost moments in time

Disappear into the night

Like wild horses that used to run

But are no longer in sight.

Friends that have gone away

Or lovers that have been lost.

Clocks steal everything,

Even when there's a high cost.

The atlas to my heart

Has been torn;

I'm lost

Without a map

To lead the way.

If you had an atlas

Of my mind,

You'd already know that

There's a lot of curves and

    broken roads ahead;

And secret messages to be

Found, made, and read.

February 6, 2020

My mind's ritual

Is comprised of

Mazes and games:

     all non-conforming, and

Non-compliant with my doctor's

Recommendations.

But who's to say

What's really going on

Inside my head?

No ritual or routine

Will stop my mind

From spinning.

Floating images

Will always be

In my periphery--

A constant reminder of possible

psychosis.

February 7, 2020

No longer enchanted

    by fairytales

    and pixie dust:

Taken over by green Martians,

Shadows, and paranoia;

               Mental breakdown—

Lost memory

And lost mind.

February 8, 2020

Like a mule with scoliosis,

Burrowing down a ravine

    and

    Carrying too much weight,

My mind is wrought with angst

Thick enough to easily

    break--

        Worrying, panicking, hurting.

There will be no picnics

    In this enchanted,

    illusory

        lifetime.

February 9, 2020

Strolling In the midnight wind

Carrying a red umbrella

Dressed in black

Wanting to sing with pride

To tell those who slumber

That insomnia's

Killing me

February 10, 2020

Under the pale full moon

Sky purple at midnight

I make one request

Of my insomniac mind:

Enjoy the light in the dark—

And work to be

The light in the dark.

February 11, 2020

Hurting, lost, and unavailable

Cannot wrap my mind around

This madness within

But the mirror does not distort—

Look what mania's done to my eyes!—

My soul gone with reality;

Dreams are my only allies.

February 13, 2020

Alone

Under the full moon I feel alright;

But, I'm stopping the search

For my sanity

Because I've lost

My light

After searching

High and low,

In rain and snow,

Only to find

Pure madness

In plain sight.

After quiet contemplation

About my dyskinetic ways

I've decided to walk with the Sun

And start enjoying my days.

So don't judge mental illness

Because you've no idea

How difficult this is.

But I'm trying, working hard

Just to live.

Through the haze of my emotions

I judge others for their own notions.

But, I'm recognizing

That we're all strange and beautiful

    creatures,

Some of whom have no one to

    impress.

So I've decided to take it easy

For not everyone can be so crazy.

I've got a home,

Not an empire

Where I can run free

Or be as mad as I'd like to be.

It's soft and cozy, though,

And love blooms like weeds.

Family runs through it

And friends do, too.

But there's no saying what

My mind will do.

There's an empire,

A corporation built,

On other's pain

And suffering. But

You can't get rid of mental illness

With strength of will,

So pharmaceuticals it is; and

My livelihood's been killed.

I want to create my own empire

Where I can feel the music

And the dead meet with the living

Where droughts don't exist

And neither does mental illness

Where strength of will cures addiction

And dark can be changed to light

Without restriction

February 15, 2020

The new moon—

A rookie this time around—

Tried to parody the Sun

To no avail.

It only made the fireball angrily

Stay around for longer days,

Burning those civilians who

      rarely sleep.

Copper irises turn to Ochoa yellow

As everything becomes nothing.

And my mind parodies Tartuffe

As it often believes I'm better.

Despite pouring rain hail,

There's still something

    to look forward to:

The flowers will return.

February 16, 2020

Echos in the mirror

Weird madness inside

Denouncing my professional creed

Retiring to uselessness

Without a sense of pride

Craving normalcy,

Wanting to cleanse my weird,

    ill mind.

Despite attempts to exceed

    past expectations,

My societal creed losing out

To madnesses' pull on my old gifts.

With only a few weird crumbs of

information about my mind

I've already realized that my

creed at normalcy is lost

Insomnia or nightmares

nothing's ever the same

Echos in the mirrors haunt me

like the ringing in my ears

To harness by my anxiousness

And critical self-doubt

I skip dinner in hopes of

   Going without

A weird spell, to be sure,

   Making things worse

But my mind's creed is no longer

   Sanity's calm.

Sliding sideways

Through loopholes in time

I realize how much has passed

And how much I've missed

While trying to avoid my

    Mental illness—

I've lost out on so much

By trying to avoid the inevitable.

Practical beauty,

But kind of weird

Lost creed and direction

When mental illness

Flipped me upside down.

Now hiding behind a disguise,

Pretending while the Sun is out;

Though I find the stars and moon

more comforting.

Constantly on the verge of madness,

But when it comes to delusions

I'm past the point of no return.

Taped up by society's norms,

And counting the hours till

    nightfall.

When I'm comfortable in my

    insanity, and if not

At least I can retire to my bed.

Too cold to gaze at the moon and
  stars,
Thinking about what could be.
So I sit inside, staring at the wall,
Wondering what could have been?

I weep, I grieve

For my mind and its illnesses--

Past the point of no return

Unsteady.

Ahead of the curve

Gifted

Until I began to

    Slide sideways

Through the loophole

    Of time's unkind curse—

Blooming psychosis

    Delusions and paranoia—

All compounded by my IQ;

Mixed emotions and a flat affect

    Followed.

Craving normalcy,

Wanting to cleanse my weird,

    ill mind.

Despite attempts to exceed

    past expectations,

My societal creed losing out

To madnesses' pull on my old gifts.

February 17, 2020

Mirror with no reflection

Loneliness dissected

Death brings out the best

    And worst of people

Grief and greed

Go hand-in-hand

Pain tampers with

Other's mechanisms

Like a bird who didn't fly south
   for the winter
The black sheep stuck without
   a lamb
Sadness consumes my being
Hurting and lonely
Greed overtakes my thinking
Exhumation will be my only relief

Reaching out for a star to sit on

Another galaxy befitting to

Wonder what it means

    To sell your soul

Prescriptions infiltrate my body

    And I question

Whether there's anything left

    On this side of worlds

February 23, 2020

Tormented by unrelenting

Emotional conundrums

And twisting physical trauma

Pain and injury to my organs

Breaking down my body

   Bit-by-bit

Losing control

Gaining regrets

A life fully lived but

No longer able to cope

Never really had #peace

Until now (that I'm gone).

Trying to keep the peace,

But simply enabling deviant behavior.

Being manipulated for control,

Tiptoeing around self-described

    royalty,

Overextending myself in the process.

Control is a powerful drug—

One I want no part of.

Exhausted and burned out;

No longer treating inconsiderates
like royalty.

Working on creating lengthy
boundaries

So I can get the peace I so desire.

Tormented by unrelenting

Emotional conundrums

And twisting physical trauma

Pain and injury to my organs

Breaking down my body

   Bit-by-bit

Losing control

Gaining regrets

A life fully lived but

No longer able to cope

Never really had peace

Until now (that I'm gone).

February 24, 2020

Highly intelligent and beautiful,

Her father's belle, though

She can't tell heaven from hell—

Unable to navigate through life

Unable to understand her mind.

Now that he's gone

Reality's non-existent;

She's no answers as to why,

Leaving an anxious mess behind.

With time and heartbeats
   fading
Loved ones leaving
Rules broken
And limits pushed,
The possibilities
Of my mind
Extend
To a world other than our own—
Where spirits and those past
Exist on a dimension slightly
   above our own,
Watching over us.

I imagine a circumstance

Where spirits exist

Where loved ones

   Never leave

Where ghosts pay visits

And old friends play

   tricks on me.

The possibilities are

   endless.

February 25, 2020

My personal vices and madness

Keep me from experiencing peace

My mind's iniquities on high alert

Wickedness runs through my veins

Spirits try and keep me safe

But the debauchery in insanity's

    Too much fun.

As time & heartbeats coincide

Spirits visit from the other side

With dirty storms of words flung

Unable to go or come

Stuck in a battlefield of empty souls

Restless or so I'm told

With zero shades of moxie left &

Their chance at peace bereft

February 26, 2020

Invisible vermin of society

Lowly souls with no hope

Off a cliff without a rope

Wrought with madness or

Down on their luck—But

Maybe it's the other way around

Freedom & happiness their gift

Souls who know something we don't

Judgement our personal vice

Invisible vermin

Play a friendly game

Only they understand

While society misunderstands

Their mind's capabilities

So, we raise the stakes

From our solitary lives

And pretend to be stuck

In space lanes

And backwater moons

February 27, 2020

Invisible mental illness

Has taken over

   my mind

Forest green martians

Now run my life

If not for prescription

I'd be paranoid all the time

But who's to say which world

   is best?

Because I sure get a lot done

   without any rest

Raising the stakes &

Playing an invisible friendly game

With those called vermin

Teasing out misunderstandings Existing in the distance

Where stars sit & observe

We laugh psychotically

& talk to spirits

Without any tangible evidences

Of mental illness

Destination unknown

When my mind reels

   With staggering thoughts.

Bewildered by which way to go

And whose voices to listen to—

A gift of mental illness

Keeps me terrified,

Or maybe I'm just on another side,

Stuck

Until my next stop—

Highs & lows my new fight.

Interactions ceased

Manipulation's gone on too long

No more friendly games

Violent words necessitate

  boundaries

Toxic environments left behind

Let me go so I can unwind

Destination unknown

New path to be forged alone

February 28, 2020

Happenstance can easily earn

Deathly ideation

Dreams of ending pain

Created by circumstance

Movement to the next world

May or may not leave you bereft

Death a becomes a gamble

A questionable friendly game

Into unknown destinations.

Decide whether bipolar disorder is

   A gift or a curse—

Because statistics say it's a deathly

   Title earned.

Ending marriages and lives

When the pain's unbearable

And the fun of mania stops,

Insomnia creeps in and

Death by depression is the end.

Solitaire & hurting

The invisible angel

Went to a dark space—

"Damage me," he said

Raising the stakes

Drowning in chemicals—

Earning his deathly title

Cascading away from pain

Into space-lanes & backwater moons

No one in the mirror

Invisible and quiet

But it's unmasking

Past the sylvan veil

Where tears echo

Strange tales

An isolated angel who sings

Damage Me with melodious

Deathly delight

February 29, 2020

Existing on different planets—

Your reality one of toxicity—

Violent words thrown &

Repeatedly stabbed too deep.

But I absorb your misunderstandings,

Wounds are created that forever seep.

So I purge myself of your negative energy &

Tears echo with melodious delight.

Stuck in a lonely world of multi-dimensions, where spirits mock my violent self-image.

Tormented by a vast emptiness inside, yet unable to purge racing thoughts out of my circular mind.

Oddly comforted by recurrent nightmares; peace remains an unlikely affair.

March 1, 2020

Only on a coastline

With indented water

Do I rabidly coexist

With raven black memories

Of throwing out my possessions

And feeling like an imposition

As I drown in chemicals

Bridging disfigured norms

And my mind's storms

March 2, 2020

There were blossoms on the tree

Next to the Atlantic in January

In the moonset darkness

When he said: Before I go

& leave this aching body behind

Know that I'm not banished

I'm favored yet lost

In between worlds

Look for me

Through the cracks in the night

& I'll be there

Beyond indented water

Over the body of the Atlantic

In a cyclone of misfortune

Pained and played

Becomes just another yesterday

So before I go, know:

I love you.

March 3, 2020

Beyond indented water

When there're whitecaps in the Atlantic

In the moon-sea darkness

Look for a falling star

In the raven black night

& know that it's me

Making sure you're alright

There will be many uncharted tomorrows ahead

But you'll be alright

Without me

My mind banished

I rabidly coexist with reality

Through the cracks in the night

When insomnia keeps me

Dancing in the dark

My disfigured truth becomes clear

Favored yet lost

Among other falling stars

And nothing is alright anymore

Life's gone dark as the raven black sky over the Atlantic at night.

Beliefs and faith broken,

Answers unspoken.

And when I tried to follow you into heaven, I was told it was before my time—all access denied.

March 4, 2020

Wishing you

Weren't taken by chaos, and,

At least, felt a few footprints of love

Before you died to live forever

In night fallen echos

And extrinsic whispers in the wind.

March 5, 2020

Wishing you were here

To share in conversation

Insanity's symphony we shared out of
relation

To take the merest breath

& compare notes of madnesses' mystery

Instead you left

No resistance, no hesitation

And I pay tribute to your liberation

March 16, 2020

My mind wandering

When the darkness rose

Now it's stagnant—no ebb and flow—

Locked inside and born of chaos

Makes looking away easier

Than confronting madness

March 17, 2020

An age of hurried stillness...

You'll find her in the treehouse

A visualization of her own making

Her mind's way of hiding

From experience she'd rather forget

And when the robots of her imagination
ebb and flow

She'll contain them in the bird house next
to it

You'll find her in the treehouse

When becoming unstable

Locked inside

When crowled demons

Ebb and flow

Born of chaos

When the darkness rose

Facing insurmountable odds

Overcoming unfathomable pain

An ancient soul

Of compassionate nature

Locked inside words

Of a narcotic rage

Like a mannequin without legs

Until a single strand of hope

Whispered my name

Tilted mercury and

Pulled my pain away

Born of chaos

Left in darkness

Becoming unstable was my fate.

But when a single strand of dim light

Whisperer my name,

My ancient soul—

Unholy but pure—

Decided to tilt mercury

Back the other way.

March 18, 2020

Find her in the treehouse

Talking to a blue bird

About kindergarten's reprieve

An ancient patient soul

Compassionate nature

Ruined by

Not just a single strand of chaos Narcotic rage witnessed

Now locked inside the unknown

March 19, 2020

Ancient soul of compassionate nature

Tried to paint my pain

When it whispered my name

But it turned black when tilting mercury

Like an armada of uncertain outcomes

That enveloped a single strand of fear & strength

Left wandering & darkness

Replaced a familiarity of loneliness

The same blue jay meets me

Outside my back door each evening

As if he's my conscience

Gently reminding me of the armada of tasks
left in the day

But for a brief moment

He takes the clock

Stops the time

Ends the pain

If only for a second

March 20, 2020

Organized my thoughts—

The echos of empty hours,

The familiarity of loneliness—

When an awakening arose

Thru cosmic energy, and

Rainy day sunshine

Reminded me of the

Bliss in consciousness.

March 24, 2020

Traveling thru time on high emotion

Oblivious to demonic dark arts

Dared to enter somewhere new

Where storks won't even appear Rather
breathe sadness

Than give my away my solitude

Orchid dreams & starry nights gone

Traded to explore mysterious

Enchanted forest of lost whispers

I dreamt of a crow—

He visits in times of grief and misfortune—

In my burdened panic

I complained,

"No matter how strong I get,

The stronger I have to become!"

He looked around my messy house,

Told me to stop with the self-pity,

Let it go; cause birds fly anyway.

March 25, 2020

As I breathe sadness

And reject the embrace of solace

My mind is quite cozy

Amongst lost whispers

And beyond the known

Entertaining madness and it's quirks

Oblivious to the dark arts

Of psychosis and mental illness

Her story:

Why be strong?
Why go on?

To seek truth?
Knowledge is given to us.
Seeing truth occupies mind's time
Before we die and
Are planted under starry nights.

Despite high emption,
An over-active nervous system,
Questions and answers I'm oblivious to,

Birds fly anyway.

March 26, 2020

I had a delicious blue dream

Where I felt the embrace of solace

As I was told there's no afterlife

But the gentle wings of a blackbird

Reminded me of the invisible barrier

I feel existing between us

Despite death's sense of separation

March 28, 2020

A crow of the blackest hue lands on top of
my bay window, as of perching on top of his
own home.

I'm living in his birdhouse, though he
doesn't seem to mind.

Then he leaves me in self-isolation, and it all
goes quiet.

I rub my eyes when I realize

More than dreams take place

In the fifth dimension

A place so close, yet so far apart

Where an invisible barrier

Separates my world from yours

All I can do is exist

In the silent blackness

That is mental illness

Until all goes quiet.

March 29, 2020

Seen and invisible barriers all around;

An overwhelming sense of

separation

Between us--

We're so close yet so far apart--

But can you feel me

As I breathe sadness

And spiral into the blackest hues of

depression?

April 15, 2020

If ever there were a time when, it's now
A wistful interlude
Upon which to tumble semi-freely
Through grief.

Until learning
A ghost of a melody
Won't present itself
Fearing continuing bonds.

A six-string rhapsody
Develops in my mind
Singing note by note
Overwhelming my emotions.
As I learn I'm now alone.

Then, a dandelion appears.

Maybe a hello?

This, I'll never know.

More than a pocketful of sighs

fill the day.

Suffocating,

Tumbling through morning clouds--

Hoping for little dreams of you,

Holding onto faint memories,

Tortured by questions unanswered—Never to

experience serenity in blue

again.

If ever there were a when it's now:

Amongst the morning clouds,

Tumbling through loss—

You left behind a pocket full of sighs

      And unanswered questions

And aren't even seen in little dreams.

Though the birds still talk of you.

Don't they?

April 16, 2020

I was enjoying

Obtuse morning clouds

Until a large cow

Knocked my serenity down

I think my smoke bothered him

The doves moved around the corner

But constant tumbling

In anguished misery

I look back

In desolation

Of paper dreams ripped up

And where my journey's brought me

If ever there were a when it's now--

Hiding from desolation

Running from repression

Yet left with a pocketful of sighs--

Anguished I resign

Though I still fear the wolf in sheep's

clothing

Lurking in the shadows

Oddly anticipating my next mistake

Desolation:

Are the voices

Simply a six-string rhapsody?

Ghosts of melodies

Observed as I passed?

I burnt them to the ground--

extinguished each, note by note.

Journey halted

Monachopsis slightly feign

Finally.

(And, hopefully, never again).

A half-empty handful of stardust

And a pocketful of sighs,

Self-pity & isolation,

Intensified my desolation.

Maybe certain memories

Are meant to fade into the darkness,

Forgotten,

Repressed for a reason.

April 17, 2020

Arrested by summer love, a tardis kept in tandem

Whispered away from the fleet and their wistful interlude

Though the ghost of a melody are indicative of the end

Of our other-worldly being

April 18, 2020

Arrested in an error of pandemonium--

Obtuse minds will never understand

A bird who can no longer fly,

Stuck in a prolific blue TARDIS,

A wistful interlude

Filled with tandem dreams

And fairytale lies.

April 22, 2020

my lost soul

accompanied by the moon
tilted by my darkest dreams
tainted by excerpts of emotion

waiting to breathe

living in the clouds
detached and drifting in time
wearing the dead

unable to move

listening to the radio

if only to fade the static--

the ringing in my ears,

a coping mechanism

to deal with fear and traumatic

perception of experience.

This waiting to breathe

is enough to

drive me mad.

April 25, 2020

despite perseverance

among

crumbled truths,

i'm still waiting to breathe;

playing with embers and flames,

my lost soul is in decline.

but u GET me SO HiGH

that i temporarily

close the door

on my grim heart.

i guess that's just

how it is.

April 28, 2020

halfway to heaven

listening to a bird's advice

walking on eggshells

over-abundance of stimuli

yet mistily I wander

in the hands of yesterday

holding ripples of repression

while probing

the rhythm of your mind

the nature of time

is killing me:

comfort's a dream.

finite moments tainted,

and bones in the hourglass

prevent hidden ethereal

moments of trust

from flowing deeply

through my immortal soul

social quagmire for a normal life

the transience of comfort

the scent of rain

make midnight whispers

& the linear nature of time

a temporary resurrection

despite accruing bones in the hourglass

preventing anything from flowing deeply

& making memories of finite moments
inadequate

April 29, 2020

new connections

created

in my mind

an abandoned warehouse

to store

memories of Stygian speeches

& bones in the hourglass

as a coping mechanism

to keep dark & powerful

words & images

from flowing deeply

thru my being

April 30, 2020

plagued

by bones in the hourglass

mistily i wander

through industrial walls

of a securely-locked hospital

where worlds made of sweat and spit

are commonalities;

a hidden, ethereal journey

awaits my release;

May 1, 2020

unable to unwind--in the middle

of holding tightly

onto ripples of memories--

just as trees breathe

mistily i wander--a journey in the hands of
yesterday--

a ragpicker crawling the wastelands

for comfort in dark medicine

escaping the mundane

during tequila sunsets w/the devil

May 2, 2020

Are we born wrong?

Attempting to escape the mundane

Eternally, we run to dark medicine:

Unwinding at tequila sunsets,

Making wishes & curses,

With the devil or a muse,

Frequently crawling the wastelands,

Seeking comfort,

Freedom from pain.

May 3, 2020

as trees breathe & blossoms bloom
hidden ethereal demons find me
when no one's around

baked in dark medicine
crawling the wastelands
frolicking by lanterns

ripples, holding the hands of yesterday,
implicating delicate memories
& patterns observed

The dint of letting go lost,
Devil or muse?

May 4, 2020

unable to withstand the test of time;

i'm stuck in inky pools of bathos

among waste & barren stone,

quivering

with each last twist of the knife;

my demons now take me

on an empty vessel

into the cold, dark emptiness.

i remember when things

didn't cause so much grief

when I stood over the darkness

not under it

unburdened by breaking boundaries

when I could free myself

when I could breathe

May 14, 2020

Beauty in death doesn't exist.

I asked the ghost-maker to take me outside
of reality anyway—where pain & toxins
don't exist.

He let me fall for fragile reflection about my
eagerness to hack dreams like data streams
& experience pain for my nocturnal sins.

May 26, 2020

i sit in my backyard

listening to the fountain breathe

through the wind song

Remembering who you were

Thinking about my anger

towards you

why did you leave me?

why did you go?

Do bodies have souls?

This we may never really know.

July 16, 2020

Death leads to eternal nothingness

Spiritually ensnared in suspected deceit

An anathema many try to avoid

Endless dream of pain, smoke & shadows

Causing harm from the allusion of
conservation

And a splintered reality doesn't even exist.

July 17, 2020

Bamboozled

By the philosophy of emotion

Desperate

In the pursuit of love, familiarity

Ensnared

By the brilliance

Of smoke and shadows

Stuck

Within honeycomb walls

Caught

In a splintered reality

Orbiting

In an endless dream

July 19, 2020

Ensnared of smoke and shadows

Orbiting inside an endless dream

Obscurity bright with empathy

A splintered reality

Whispering your name

Permitting brief calm through deceit

Surrender without peroration

July 21, 2020

Orbiting

As heartstrings weep

Quietly yelling

While dreaming of a dream

Fatally experiencing

Fortune's fate

Waiting

To be taken away

And returned

To my part time life.

July 22, 2020

Orbit the passage to tomorrow

Accompany the unruly & untamed

Crash & burn behind a mask

Inconspicuous ethereal conjuring

Beyond the pavement—

The fatal final note—

Take away fortune's fate

Heartstrings weep for my last song

Dream of a dream refreshed w/glory.

August 12, 2020

Someone whispered in the dark

Empyreal or divergent from

The voices in my head?

Enchanted flickers of light

Revealed shadows of memories

Brought wistful reverie

Of unalloyed sentiment

A smile to remember.

August 19, 2020

Flickers of de ja vu

As I sleep less & less

Ready to put you to rest

A lone howler of lightning & thunder

Vital inflection of next time

Leads to artful composition—

Sing me a song, a prologue of contravariant
salvation,

As I bury your velveteen bones

In the chassis of time.

August 23, 2020

Hidden saltwater pebbles, tears

Pressed between chapters

Bemused battlefields reenacted

No net in the forecast

Drawn deeper into revulsion

Until awakened by gossamer

Dreams—ethereal nightmares

Under iridescent clouds—

Bewildered vice written

On the soul: survival

Without comfort.

August 24, 2020

Distinctively drawn

By the odor

Of intoxicated sin

Reminds me

There's no reward

Beyond existentialism

In the velvet debris

Of death.

Still, I avoid smashing bumblebees—

Consciously maintaining survival

As tears & meteors fall

From heaven

In enigmatic minutes

I don't remember.

August 30, 2020

Shadows playing tricks

On my fractured mind

Guiding me through

Another time

Diluted memories

Not forgotten

My bones still ache

And my heart still breaks

Through the finity of smoke

Pain remains

And everything's still the same

A unique mess of energy

Made unstable by

Whispers never shared.

Echoing footsteps

Consume

My fractured mind.

Watching, wishing,

I was imagining

Another time.

August 31, 2020

Driftless reflections of me

Tangled among fractal clouds

Until the heft and weight

Pull me down from

Unique and picturesque

Glory of ink that heals.

Unblinking, forged by fire,

No longer feeling the words of

A safe passage—

Trapped in my mind

Far from society

Where stories live.

Fractal memories

Watering my dreams,

Driftless, forgetful—

Paper thin

Comprehension of

Ink that heals—

Forged by fire,

Tangled,

Far from any

Safe passage

Out of this pain;

United with

The unblinking

Heft and weight

Of

Reflections of me.

September 1, 2020

Obsessing over

Powerful insults

Catapulted;

Feeling the heft

And weight

Of veritable anger

In maligned words

Vetted over,

And over, again—

Unable to keep my heart safe,

Unable to hide from the pain—

Trapped On a tightrope in a breeze;

Stuck on the surface

Of what cuts

The heart.

September 16, 2020

Spellbound by
Beautiful contradictions
Until unexplainable

Realizations of hidden
Truths permeate
The psyche.

Dreams in colour
Cease to exist, in an
Unfounded search for light:

But only diabolical
Dialogue illuminates
Perpetual penance.

Spellbound by unexplainable spectacles of illusion, and

The unseen thrumming from beyond the moon,

Dreams in colour cease to exist:

Disaster hovers beautiful

Contradictions, and unexplainable

Realizations that we're no longer united permeates the psyche.

Only left with soulless words, and

Diabolical dialogue, which Illuminates hidden truths,

We're left afraid and alone—

Stuck in an unfounded search for Starlight, though

Trapped in a blind Vault of scorched,

135

Perpetual penance.

September 18, 2020

Privy

To the past we left behind,

Searching

For light in the dark; but

There's no heaven

For the spellbound

With so many faces—

Useless, flimsy words

Scorch and invoke trouble,

Holding us hostage—

Unable to resonate

With the life and

Heart we once knew.

October 13, 2020

Naked, wide open

Ephemeral yet lithe

Thoughts in flight

A hue of ravens

With wings of blood

Hollow voids

In my blackened

Murderous heart

Conviction bleeds

Beneath misgiving

In an insane asylum

To coalesce

Behind the mirrors

Of a labyrinth trail

Of reflected truth

October 15, 2020

Insane resignation to

Spells and spirits

Summoning gone wrong

Beyond the smoke

Thirteen echos ache

Ephemeral hollow voids

More than lithe dents

In blackened winds

Coalesce in resignation

Darker than death

Only in the autumn

Unkind memories and

Reflected truths become

Tricks of

Snarling chills and

Barren crypts

Of grief.

Bent beneath fear,

Eerie creatures

Bare their souls;

Haunted,

Unsettled, and

Unable to demystify

Their ominous path.

October 17, 2020

Haunted by betrayal

Darker than death

In a wasteland

Beyond the pines

Aching

Tasting the pain

Unable to take hold

Of questions never asked

October 20, 2020

Betrayed beneath

Inescapable

Death defying

Malevolence laid bare

Ashes transform

Branded by fire

Distressed

Burned

Crawling

Ominous aura

Ephemeral effigy

Lithe duplicity

Searching for

Words that echo

Whispers in the stitching

October 21, 2020

Alone in the night

Obfuscatory nightmares

Leave inescapable scars

Frozen beneath

Swallowed incisions

Invisibly bleeding

In a rouge wasteland

Forged by fire

Betrayed by duplicity

Malevolence laid bare

Death inside the devil's shadow

October 27, 2020

Only in the autumn

Unkind memories and

Reflected truths become

Tricks of Snarling chills and

Barren crypts

Of grief.

Bent beneath fear,

Eerie creatures

Bare their souls;

Haunted,

Unsettled, and

Unable to demystify

Their ominous path.

Haunted by betrayal

Darker than death

In a wasteland

Beyond the pines

Aching

Tasting the pain

Unable to take hold

Of questions never asked

October 28, 2020

Beliefs undone

Hope gone

Numinous experiences

Miles away—

Through the shadows weave

Dark illusions

Stuck in the other, the unknown,

Pressing deeper

Into the darkness—

Wake me up

When it's over.

October 31, 2020

Under the full blue moon

On hollow's eve

A eulogy

Within earshot, and a

Graveyard made.

Nightmares and

Dreams eclipsed,

No longer pressing

Deeper

Into the darkness—

Letting go.

And maybe tomorrow

Death will evoke transformation,

And in the aftermath,

Golden silence.

November 9, 2020

Surrounded by

Crushing silence,

Dark shadows

Loom

In the periphery.

Ungrounded—

Falling backwards,

Outside the boundaries

Of sanity—

On pins and needles,

With bated breath,

Words fail.

As the smoke rises

And the snow falls

In a cult of technicalities,

Give the devil his due.

Or his blight of pain

Will freeze the mind

And he'll

Never

Meet his end.

November 18, 2020

'alone by the circus'

actions and reactions
never resolved

expressed too little or
too much emotion

still suffering inside
out

heightened amplified senses
unable to rest

over-pushing achievement

unremarkable

giving up—crashing
afraid to sleep

November 20, 2020

Stuck on the edge of torment

Enveloped in wistful remorse

Sundown on easy street

Doesn't exist

Maybe tomorrow

Suffering will dissipate

Fractured by life's game

Consumed in numbing pain

Faltering

Lost

Unable to smile

Unable to heal

Floating in circles

Around a museum of memories

November 23, 2020

within

the silent

language of sighs,

lacking in strength,

(unable to look in the mirror),

falling in the folds

of nothingness

to the depths

of solitude.

December 25, 2020

brilliance in insight

challenging, disputing

every action, every word,

every sight, every smell,

every thought

of my own.

December 26, 2020

Running around the world;

No longer carrying
My resilient ribbon;

Talking in no time;

Patience wanes
In the chill of seaside dampness.

So I look up

At a single star
In the navy night sky,

In awe in hopelessness.

Madly

medicating;

Ripping thru

an influx of input:

mixed feelings,

frustration, anger, fear;

mixed actions;

cyclical thinking—

A mixed mind;

Misunderstanding.

December 28, 2020

Reflecting upon

Unexpected endings;

Mis- understanding

That which cut too deep;

Sadness forever comes and goes;

And, as you wane in the wind,

Wounds will never heal.

December 29, 2020

Surrounded by barbed wire

On lockdown in an unintelligible mind

Amongst the dust and smoke

Amongst the various birds and wet, dead leaves,

I inhale,

And forget to breathe.

December 31, 2020

as feelings of grandiosity fade

realistic expectations appear on the
horizon, and

fear embalms itself

in anticipation

of moving forward

in change

and understanding.

January 1, 2021

She, terrorized by her mind,
Me, not questioning mine,

Jumped off the ledge of a bridge
Together, hoping for the best;

Weren't there warning signs

Before she suffocated us?

January 19, 2021

A disassembled existence

Without gravity, and no sense of balance;

Missing the half-moon through the sticks
and dead leaves;

They, the stars, are watching us—though
too blurry to

find when falling through racing thoughts.

Unable to focus, to see, to stop spiraling, to
be free.

January 21, 2021

stuck in a shell of stigma

collapsing inward

questioning self-worth

quietly letting go

shedding invisible armor

beginning to breathe

silently starting to grow

slowly moving forward

dignity in tow

January 22, 2021

Consumed by a tornado of broken hearts.

Falling backwards into a very dark place.

Wondering, every day, where you went,
and why.

January 23, 2021

A salty-white dove emerged

from under the floorboards,

Reluctantly read my aura,

Told me to lighten up,

And flew away,

Alone.

January 26, 2021

Children run wild as woven elements come
together;

Esteemed parents crawl and chase
preconceptions;

Weathered, there's no dark corridor—no
hiding inside a barrier.

But, standing together, understanding the
space

between thoughts, creates a love that's
never enough.

February 9, 2021

Lackluster, disparate dispositions
Held hostage in an empty house
Of undifferentiated whispers
Without sunshine

Medication sucked up energy
Swallowed my aura
No longer a rarity
Normalcy of zombies

With suspended beliefs
My delusional heart
Hopes
For a little more light

In a graveyard of poets

Hearing undifferentiated whispers

Makes me question

If there is there an afterlife?

Or do delusional hearts

Simply go on hoping for more?

Unable to embrace inner peace

Pushing away from stillness

Glimpses of sunshine

Through the rain

Trickle the question,

"Why the resistance? The hesitation?"

To which, I climb into my sheets

And disappear into another

Nightmare.

February 12, 2021

I don't think I'll even get home—
I'm stuck in unoblivion,
Unable to take my mind off details,
Never missing a thing.
Overly preoccupied,
I'll never traverse this maze.

February 13, 2021

Building a bridge between

Reality lost

And feigned anxiousness;

Reconciling

Differences in understanding;

Compromising,

To a manageable degree.

February 14, 2021

In a tornado of broken hearts

Misery in lackluster nerves

Mistakes and words to overcome

That falling feeling signifies

The end of the road

Time to step into the future

No more rose petals dripping red

Long lost hope of self-love

And fire beneath feelings

Become reality.

February 15, 2021

Words fall with raindrops
Skeletal flowers present themselves
Content attachments come apart
My rare aura offers a little more light
Poetry flourishes on rainy days
As broken sunsets fall into night.

I know I'm going manic
When I get creative;
But that's my favorite part
Of my being.

Paranoid by the hidden moon;

Preoccupied by whispering voices;

Thoughts take over the room.

Living asymmetrically,

Aura

Upside down & inside out,

Heartbroken & defeated,

I keep climbing—

I can't stop moving—

Circumstance

Intentionally forgotten

Don't pull me out of insanity.

February 16, 2021

Walking pavements

Frantically wondering

Which way is up—

Nothing's in the right place—

Spinning into unconsciousness

Distorted dreams of reality

Run through my veins,

Making waves with

    a sharpened knife.

February 17, 2021

Standing still in a linear world

Gave away cherished property

Over-poured my ego

Until I couldn't breathe

Exhilarated, Intoxicated,

Detached, Embarrassed—

My abilities keep fighting with me.

February 18, 2021

Rainy day lovers

Unwrapped at warped speed

Excited, no longer inhibited

Vices & judgements forgotten

Consciousness unchained

Inebriated among the haze

Stomach in knots, panic

But is it wrong?

My dear muse.

February 19, 2021

Surrounded by butterflies

Sought ethereal calmness

Craved attention

Choked into darkness

Obsession

So hold gently my neck

And never let go

February 20, 2021

Connecting through crazy stories

Past mud left to dry

Through unprotected wavelengths

Vulnerable complexities, deep affection

You cracked my chest

To your vast walls of openness

February 22, 2021

Hush now, just rest

Hear the rhythm in my breath

Just as bled roses

Took the plunge

Don't fear the thorns of love

Crawl out when you're ready

Your bright energy

A riddle for humanity

February 24, 2021

Relaxed invitation to a kiss

Woven in time.

Insatiable appetite

For poetry in the dark.

Resounding the bedrock

After a feisty scratch.

Darkness controls the lovesick.

Languid? Just rest.

February 25, 2021

Silence drinks me—

Listens to the rhythm

In my breath,

Counts the vibrations

In my chest—

Ends with a goodnight kiss.

But if you can

Feel the

Pounding of

My heartbeat,

Slide off to sleep,

And just rest.

February 26, 2021

Impatiently pacing about

On the pretense

Of tactless charm.

Brooding about

The dark side

Of human nature.

All that's left

Is a folded

Shadow of you.

Who are you hiding from?

What's on fire? What's undercover?

Who are you trying to kill?

February 27, 2021

All-consuming anxiety

Rufescent winds of anger

And a languid peach fantasy

Woven through my being

Indolent in time

My mind a war machine

Silence drinks me

Even the weather isn't bipolar

March 1, 2021

Know me:

Hiding unbridled,

Scathing pain.

Know me:

Still in control,

Far from giving in.

Know me:

Abandoned time

To daydream.

Know me:

To gain relief

From suffering.

Know me:

Living among distractions,

Darkness now controls

My howling eyes.

March 4, 2021

Bound by routine
And time.

Trapped inside echoing
Conflict,

Fleeting whispers
And lies.

Fixated
On sweet insanity.

Hear the dissonance
In my voice.

Darkness controls

By shifting Light.

And pandemonium arrives.

March 20, 2021

A maelstrom of sensations

Erupted in waves

Of broken and vivid yesterdays;

History bruised

And paradise lost—

The effects of actions

Have high costs.

March 28, 2021

Overcome the fear

Of being locked away

Go beyond time

Appreciate the unexpected

Become addicted to change

Move forward in life:

"You're gonna be fine."

Maintaining equilibrium,

Whimsical relationships will end

In self-preservation

When your caring spirits,

Killer comforts and confidence,

Vulnerabilities,

And unaccustomed thoughtfulness

Isn't enough

As I shed the dark

On my classy mess

Of bones and skulls

Fighting loneliness together

Stealing comfort

By way of conversations,

Gentle interactions—

Whimsical poetry in bed.

April 4, 2021

Powerfully reserved;

Cautiously outgoing;

The silence in your eyes,

A dark fragility

From the sticky,

Midnight Sun.

May 18, 2021

Traveling among

Lost graveyards

At midnight

Keeps me spinning

Looking for memories

Of you.

May 26, 2021

Listening to and
Letting go of
Whispers in the wind—
Ignorance is no longer
Bliss.

August 23, 2021

No relief from loneliness

Nor the potent push of ongoing pain

Makes manic agitation

An apt escalation

When being trivialized,

Dismissed, and stigmatized,

For what's frequently held

And hidden inside.

August 24, 2021

Play me cruel—

Before my

Flirtatious addiction

Leaves you

In exquisite agony.

August 29, 2021

Malefic undertones

Of pressed fentanyl pills

May rid one's self

Of the pain & anxiety felt

When mental illness

Takes up home

Within one's soul,

Encompassing their entire being.

Until becoming

The nucleus of death—

There's no such thing

As opiates & ice cream.

September 12, 2021

Memories lost,

Moments stolen:

Repression in

My mind's eye—

A gusty windstorm

Of unapproximated pain

Drowning in self-doubt

And hearts re-healing

After having been

Judged and over-broken.

September 13, 2021

IF ONLY my intuition was telling me

Time was running out for

The pointlessness and uselessness

Of hurt words wrought from

Childhood overachievement sought.

September 30, 2021

Medication swallowed my energy
Dulled my aura—
No longer a rarity—existing in the
Normalcy of zombies.

Despite lackluster dispositions
When in an empty, grayed out house
Of undifferentiated whispers
Never to see the light.

Still,
My delusional heart
Hopes
For rays of sunshine.

October 5, 2021

as leaves fall and dandelions

get put to sleep

cotton candy nightmares

are kept at bay

by the beautiful ghosts

    that grace your dreams.

October 7, 2021

Spellbound, hell-bound;

Worlds a wreck — put my gut in knots!;

Shaking, changing every chance i get;

Before jumping down a well of ancient shadows;

Only to bury myself below their burned rocks.

October 29, 2021

Emotions buried deep in a dark aquarium

Until it becomes a crypt with no exits found,

A place where tangerine blush dreams
come to drown...

November 10, 2021

Promises
 broken before they're made

Peace and joy
remain out of sight

Dormant are the harmonious

November 20, 2021

To my ghosts,

Dear voices! leading me
Demanding, reprimanding
(if allowed)
Though I've tied you
Close to me,
I walk alone
As darkness unfurls
Over the salty, hazed,
Residual world,
Haunted-heart crushed,
Endlessly questioning myself,
Eternity.

November 26, 2021

Though the wind whispered goodbye

To your overactive mind,

To overlapping noise in the background,

To admonishing pain in the foreground,

I'm still here.

Stuck In the thrum of selfishness,

Wishing you'd changed

To be here with me, if in agony.

Don't trust me

In the dark,

When the thrum of time

Edges us closer,

Delectable parts

To be satisfied.

Until the owls fade

And dawn arrives.

Yet, excitement continues, if only

In titillating conversation—

We'll have a bloody good time.

December 19, 2021

I lull on the edge of forever

Trapped within rock walls

Boundaries

Said protection

Against vulnerabilities

Bruises, injuries to ego

Yet still searching

For that which I'll never find

An enigma

Poised peace

Within

My damaged, chaotic mind

December 23, 2021

The reasons are 50/50:

I was

Half-in for the fear,

Half-out for the fear.

But that's half the fun.

Is it worth the earthly ethereal vibrations experienced?

Does is it outweigh secret, silent sorrow felt inside?

Yes, cause

I was

Half-in.

January 23, 2022

I was only afraid of the devil 'til

He used his cold, dark shadow

To embrace me, so that

Vibrant strung harmonies

We're no longer heard;

In the wilderness of want,

They'd long disappeared

Even before his late arrival—

And incremental murmurs of strangulation

Were never heard.

January 25, 2022

In the detritus of winter,
 A magical twist began
Whereby my combatant mind
Began a peaceful duet together—
Fleeting yesterday,
Dripping in lucidity.

Ignoring my own

Combatant mind,

I was only existing

In a fantasy—

A world of lovers,

And ice cream delight.

January 27, 2022

Backyard sparrows — uncanny

Ghosts explode

Into lucidity;

Want,

Want to be free,

But there's too many layers

Underneath.

January 29, 2022

In love with mountainous infatuation,

When taboos beget for

Peaking highs of romantic naivety;

I crave the lowly hills,

When the better of temptation

Can go no more;

Even feeling blue,

All sympathies disregarded,

As memories melt away,

Emotional detachment remains

Forevermore.

Sleep hard to come by

Dreams amiss

Spirits no longer putting in

An appearance;

Guidance gone,

Anxiety ridden insomnia

And burned out mania

Remain—

As if I was only

A bystander,

I drift

Listening to the voices

Play.

February 10, 2022

In the usual state of panic,

Here we go again,

In a song without a melody,

Despite the kettle and mangoes,

Feelings proliferate pages—

Privacy's subdued;

I was only trying to cope.

February 16, 2022

With another bridge to perpetually cross

Hereafter echos a sane search

Albeit ignited in flames

I was only trying to get back home

But underneath lies forbidden fruit

A frail, unattainable discovery

That'll remain under suspenseful eyes

      Forevermore

As I fail and move on…

February 21, 2022

I was only there when everything

Was destroyed.

Now, the smoke

 Still lingers.

And we look for

Longer days; hope for

Brighter ways.

But there's no way

Out of this grey destruction.

February 22, 2022

Dangerous, this hollow ground

I float slightly above,

And I was only

Looking to move

My ghost

Home;

Stained-glass heart and all.

February 23, 2022

In the darn arena

Of her eyes

You could see

She would only drink

To escape, in an attempt

To get home.

But the devious smile

Upon her cheek

Told a story of one who

Remains braced where

You can't even shake

The frosted ground.

February 28, 2022

Out from under the waves

    hollow depths

Unfurled seashells

    arose

The dust settled

    and the dawn

Abode.

March 6, 2022

Be weary of

Midnight confessions and

Paper cup ink —

Unlike

Dried

Honey crumble,

Words stay.

March 31, 2022

Whimsically riding a daydream
  through reality

April 15, 2022

Desolate & alone

I inhale razor breaths

As the universe

Rakes my bones

Into discord.

After

My brain, my mind,

My being,

Turned to cabbage,

I was

Broken down

Into dust, &

My soul surrendered

To the fatality.

I was only seeking rest.

April 16, 2022

Once upon a dream,

I remember that night

Before

Your fatality.

A harrowing adventure

Cherished like

A waterfall

Made of weaving diamonds.

But, memories slip, surrender

Into the empty,

Along side

Another lost love song.

April 19, 2022

Hairs stand on end.

Chills

Restrict

My trembling body.

Kiss me.

May 7, 2022

Under the static threads of starlight

Dystopia's hollow descent

Into the limestone graveyard

Fatefully or fortunately (or both?)

Unfurled to its end

As different layers

Of reverberated communication

Mysteriously went silent.

May 20, 2022

Your attention

I craved

Your kindness

I appreciated

Your affection

I loved

My clinginess

You hated

My neediness

You despised

My obsession

You feared

June 25, 2022

My lost soul

Accompanied by the sun
Tilted by my darkest dreams
Tainted by excerpts of emotion

Waiting to breathe

Living in the clouds
Detached & drifting in time
Wearing the dead

Unable to move

July 2, 2022

Standing outside heartbreak hotel

No longer living in a dream

A tumbleweed rolled by

And a lizard over my foot

Was I always this parched?

Or did I simply dry out?

From crying too many tears?

July 17, 2022

While searching for the wonder

In our little corner of the world

Moonlight announced

Adoration of the other—

Not zombies,

But men, rather,

With total control,

In the spotlight,

Oozing of silence.

July 18, 2022

We all will face her;
Tomorrow's never promised.

Disregard their egos,
And pride of place.

Share moments
And vocalize feelings.

Live in the unique beauty
Of the unexpected.

Maintain a circle
Opposite indifference.

Slow down;

Feel the heatwave.

August 30, 2022

Stuck in insomnia

Under the moonlight

Unable to deal with this pain

Moving from room to room

Like a ghost during the day

September 28, 2022

In the silence

Beyond the empty days

Friends fall into enemies

Control is lost and

Leaves begin to rustle

In the moonlight

Of my insomnia

September 30, 2022

Sweet lullaby that doesn't exist

Rustling leaves and dying dandelions

Remind me of ghosts in our midst

Made in the USA
Middletown, DE
30 November 2022

16558424R00135